The Time of My Life

Written By: Karen Nicksich
Illustrated By: Earlene Gayle Escalona

Copyright © 2015 by Karen Nicksich. 717684
Library of Congress Control Number: 2015911149

ISBN: Hardcover 978-1-5035-8901-8
 Softcover 978-1-5035-8507-2
 EBook 978-1-5035-8506-5

All rights reserved. No part of this book may be reproduced or transmitted in any form or by any means, electronic or mechanical, including photocopying, recording, or by any information storage and retrieval system, without permission in writing from the copyright owner.

This is a work of fiction. Names, characters, places and incidents either are the product of the author's imagination or are used fictitiously, and any resemblance to any actual persons, living or dead, events, or locales is entirely coincidental.

Print information available on the last page

Rev. date: 07/22/2015

To order additional copies of this book, contact:
Xlibris
1-888-795-4274
www.Xlibris.com
Orders@Xlibris.com

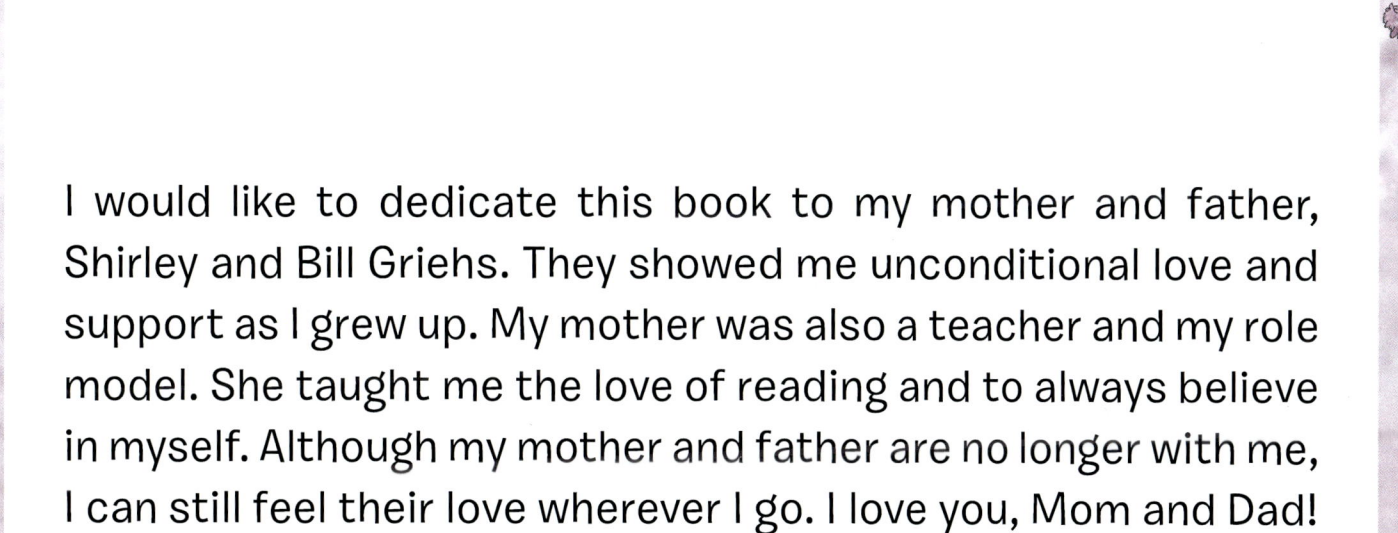

I would like to dedicate this book to my mother and father, Shirley and Bill Griehs. They showed me unconditional love and support as I grew up. My mother was also a teacher and my role model. She taught me the love of reading and to always believe in myself. Although my mother and father are no longer with me, I can still feel their love wherever I go. I love you, Mom and Dad!

The story you are about to read is based on real events. But before we begin, find a place where you like to relax and forget about any problems you may have. Now take three deep breaths—one breath at a time. Count to three in your head, and then blow the air out so slowly that only your ears can hear it. Next, close your eyes and imagine a place of love and light and happiness. It could be with your family or you holding a pet or maybe even walking in the clouds. Are you there? Perfect!

Now open you eyes and turn the page. We are ready to begin our story.

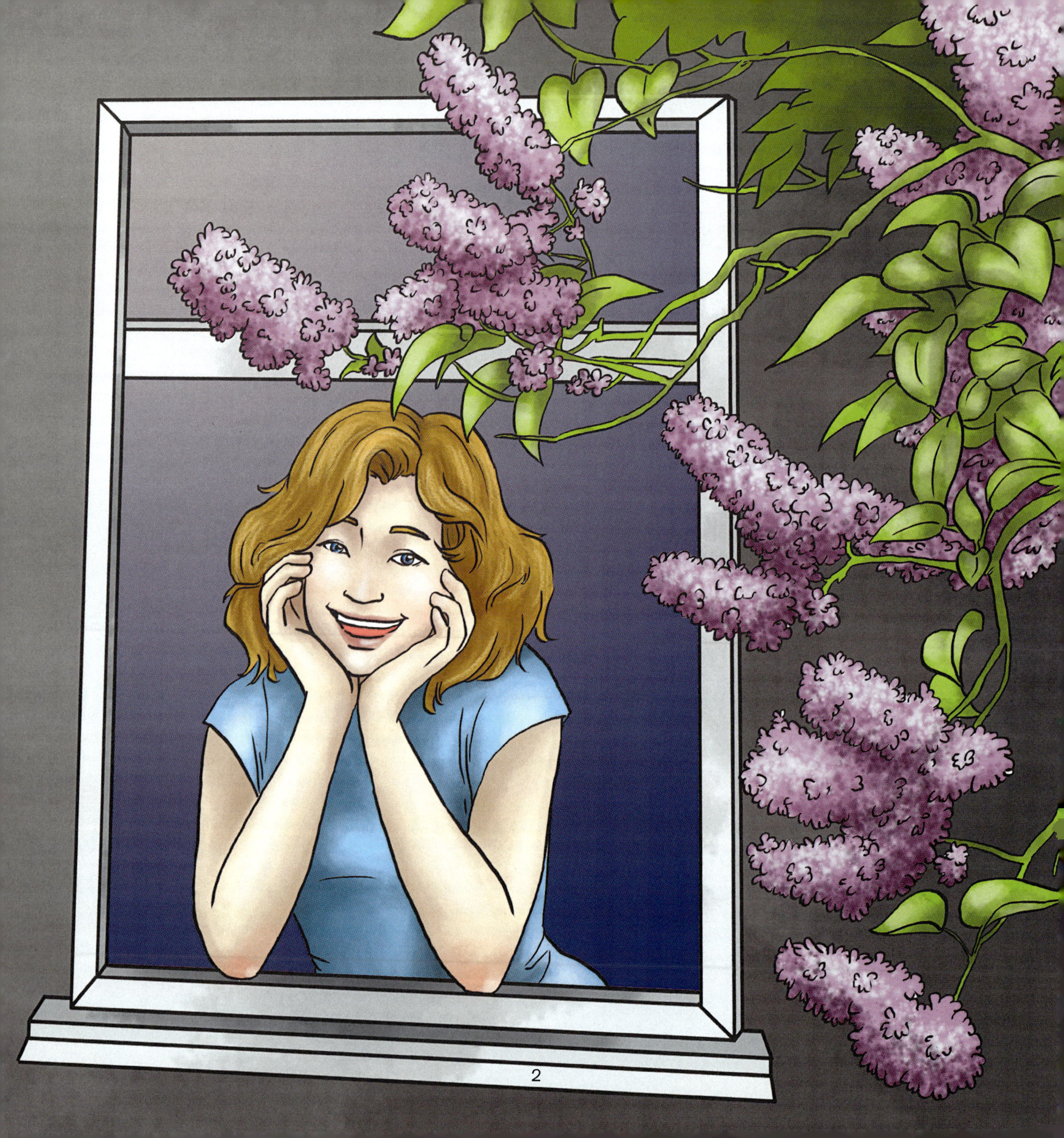

Sunrise brought in a new day at the Lilac Doggie Rescue Ranch. The sweet smell of lilacs drifted through Anna's bedroom window. Anna welcomed the day with a smile, looking out her window to see the soft purple haze of the multicolored lilacs she tended.

Anna was kind, gentle, and thoughtful. Each step Anna took was a step toward healing and rehabilitating dogs that had been abused or neglected. She dedicated her life to helping dogs without homes.

Anna's parents raised her with love. They taught her to be aware and respect everything in and on Earth. Anna learned that love has no boundaries. Often Anna would seek guidance from Mother Earth. Anna had a strong connection to nature and all those who lived there. Experiencing the splendor of what nature provided brought Anna the highest level of joy.

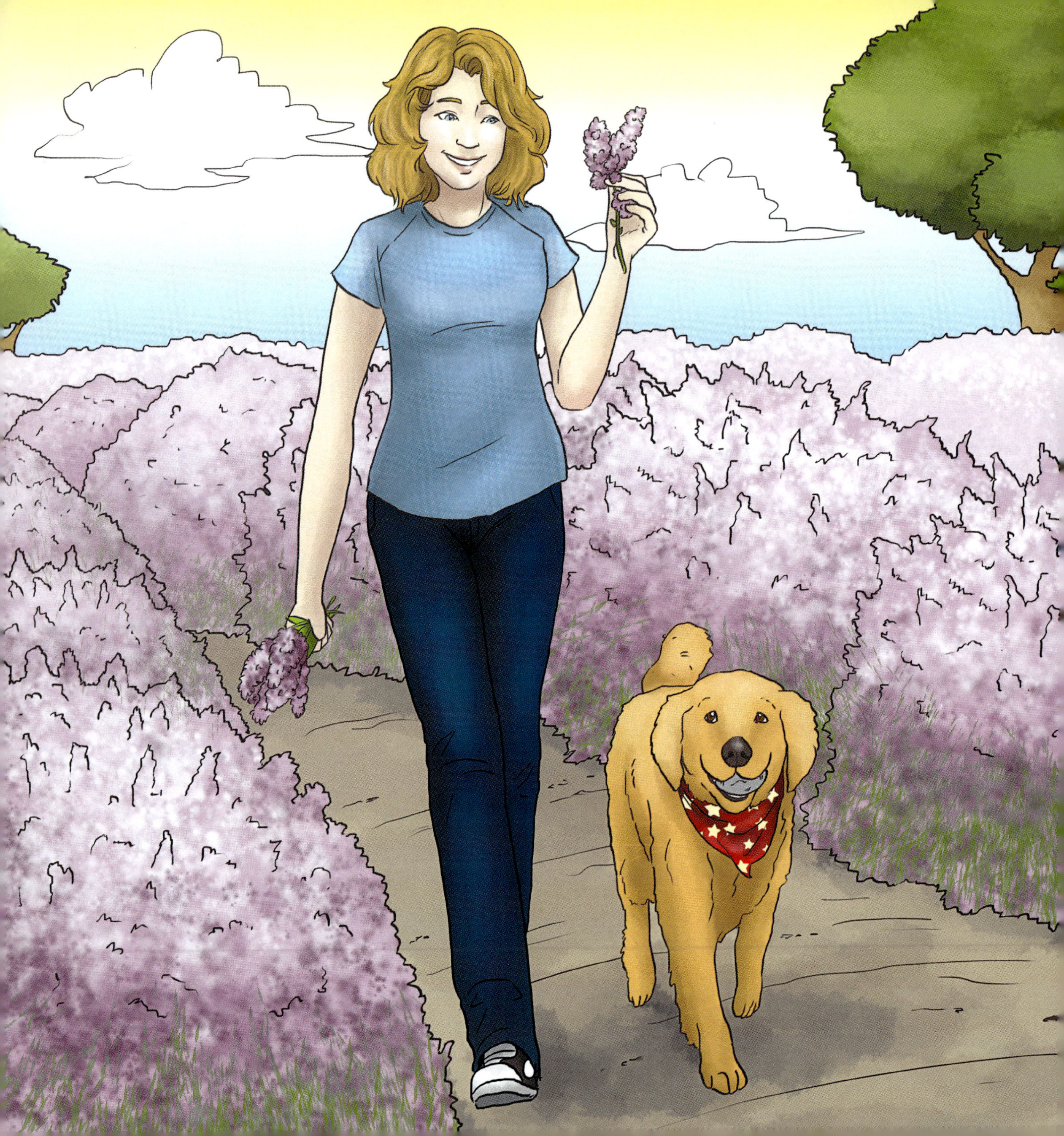

Each morning Anna greeted Max, her Golden Retriever of eleven years, by kissing his forehead and stroking his beautiful golden fur coat.

"Good morning, Max," she said. "What a good dog you are. Thank you for being in my life."

Anna prepared Max's breakfast before tending to the dogs in their home away from home.

"Let us take a walk down the path together and sit underneath the Wise Old Tree," Anna said.

Max wagged his tail in excitement, knowing this was his special time to be with Anna.

As they walked together down the path, Anna gathered sprigs of multicolored lilacs to present to the tree as a gift. Max picked up a rock to carry in his mouth.

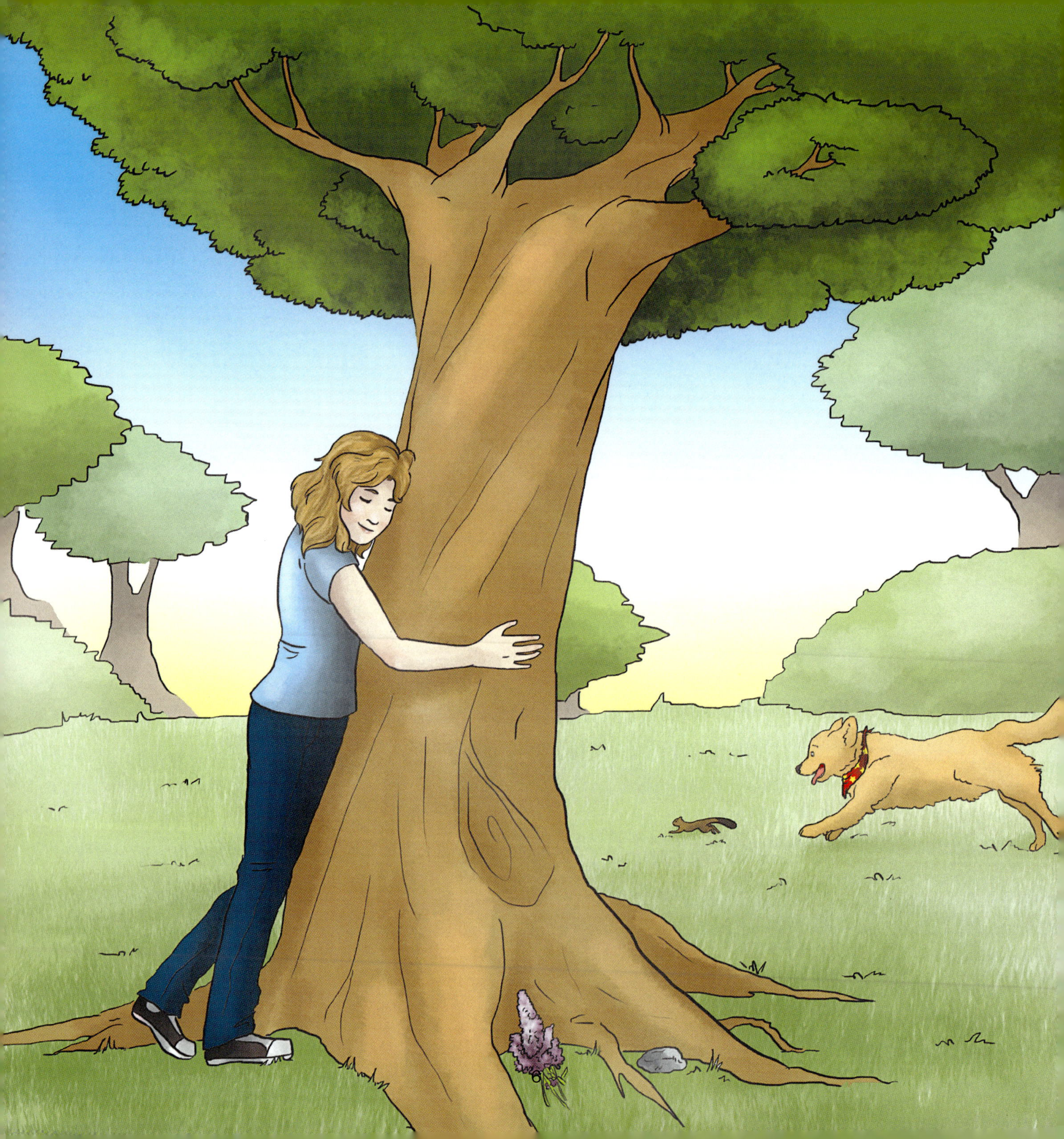

When they arrived at their destination, Anna arranged the lilacs on the ground as Max dropped his rock next to the tree. She hugged the tree as if they were old friends. Anna remembered the day that she helped her father plant the tree when she was a small child.

The tree held special memories of growing up with her parents on this special ranch for dogs. Scratched in the bark of the tree were Anna's initials. The tree helped ground Anna when she felt overwhelmed or sad.

Max and Anna sat beneath the tree to take in the beauty of the ranch and the rescue dogs that lived there.

"Life is good, Max, but we must always remember the importance of respecting and honoring what life has given us," Anna said. "We must never take it for granted."

Max pressed his paw print into the ground to mark this special spot. Then Max ran off to chase a squirrel, knowing he would never catch it.

Welcome to
Lilac Doggie Rescue Ranch
ALL WHO ENTER THIS RANCH
MUST SHOW LOVE, RESPECT
AND KINDNESS TO THE
ANIMALS THAT LIVE HERE.

Anna looked up to the tree for guidance. Not only did Anna have the gift of communicating with animals, but she also listened to what the tree had to say as her back rested against the rough bark. She took out her journal and wrote down what the Wise Old Tree told her:

- *Stand tall and be proud of who you are.*
- *Go out on a limb to help someone, be it an animal or a man.*
- *Remember your roots so that you may always be grounded, and respect what nature has given you.*
- *Drink plenty of water so that you will always be healthy.*
- *Be content with your natural beauty and that of others.*
- *Show kindness to all animals, big and small, and in return, you will teach the animals to do the same.*

Anna stood up and hugged the tree. "Thank you, Wise Old Tree," she said. "I will make a sign today to hang at the entrance of our ranch."

The sign read:

Welcome to Lilac Doggie Rescue Ranch
ALL WHO ENTER THIS RANCH MUST
SHOW LOVE, RESPECT, AND KINDNESS TO THE
ANIMALS THAT LIVE HERE.

Anna walked through the lilac fields, enjoying the beautiful colors and scent of the sweet-smelling flowers on her way to the bunkhouse where all the animals were sleeping. As she approached the entrance of the bunkhouse, Anna listened to the songbirds singing and chirping in the trees. She took in a deep breath of fresh air and opened the door to the bunkhouse.

12

Anna began to sing, *"Good morning, good morning, it's time to say hello again. Good morning, good morning to you!"*

All the dogs began to sing back to her by howling, baying, and woofing. Anna stroked the fur of the dogs and kissed the tops of their heads. All the animals, big and small, stretched their paws, claws, feathers, and hooves.

In unison, they said, "Good morning, Ms. Anna. What a glorious day it will be on our ranch today."

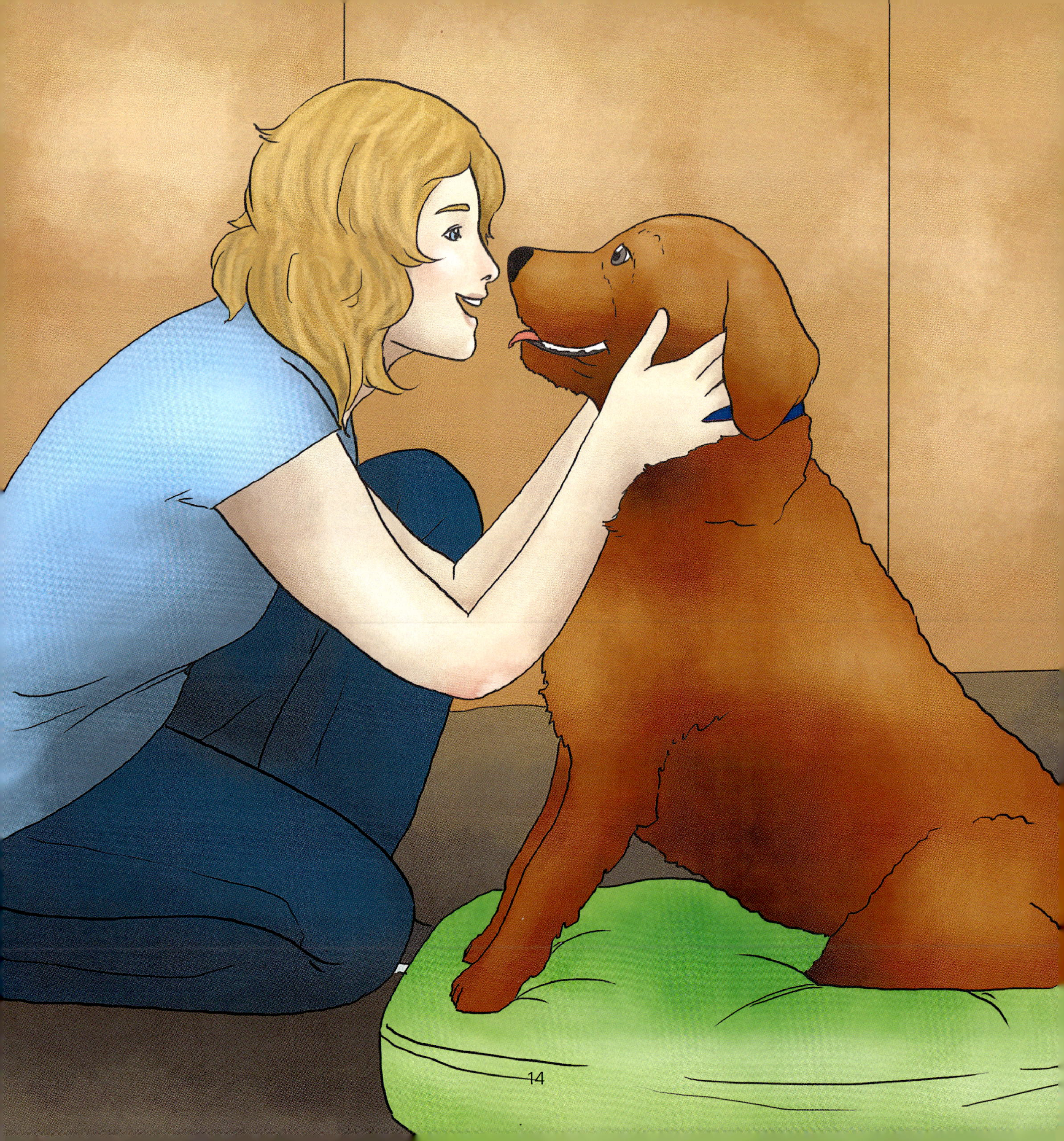

Anna walked over to Dante, her other Golden Retriever, and rubbed his deep velvet red fur. Anna had named him that because his fur was as crimson as Dante's inferno. Anna loved all her dogs, but Dante was special. She had rescued him fourteen years ago. Dante was Anna's guardian angel. It was Dante's job to watch over all the other dogs and Anna's family.

When Anna's mother and father had to go on trips, it was Dante who stood guard and watched over the other dogs and Anna until the parents came back home. Dante loved to dance to Motown music in the kitchen with Anna as she prepared the meals for all the dogs. Dante would lie on her bed when she was ill. And you could count on Dante for playing icky ball with Anna.

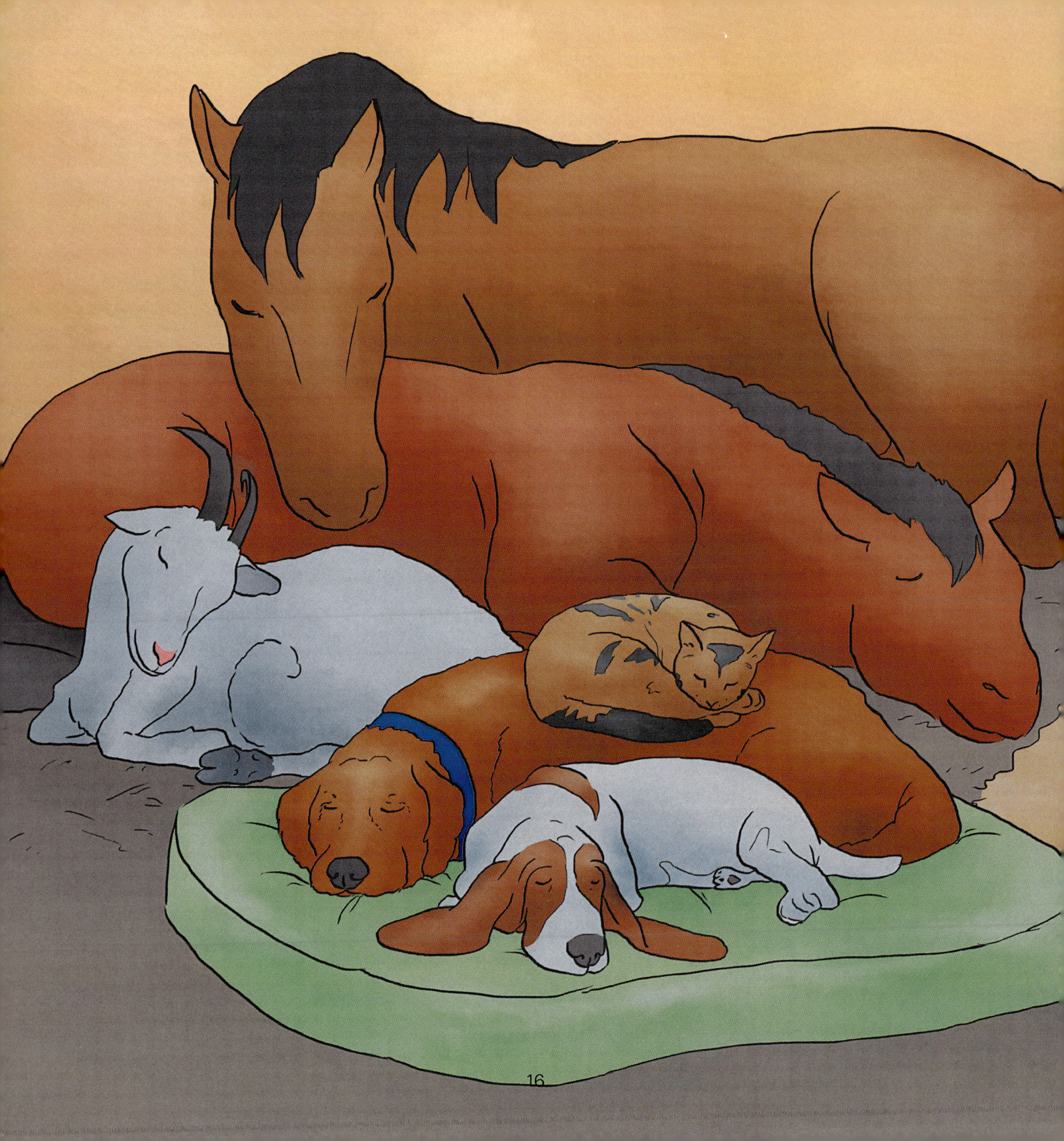

Dante had the choice of sleeping in the house or the bunkhouse. But last night Dante had stayed with the other dogs because of a severe rainstorm. He reassured the dogs who were frightened by the thunder. He invited them into his soft bed and let them snuggle. In the morning, there was a dog pile on top of Dante.

Anna had also rescued a fluffy black cat she found by the river. She named the cat Buzzy because when it purred, it buzzed like a bee. When Anna first rescued Buzzy, it hid under the refrigerator for five days. Then there was the time when Buzzy ate the entire turkey as it sat on the counter to rest. But today Buzzy stretched its slender body and walked over to a sunbeam that was coming through the door to sun.

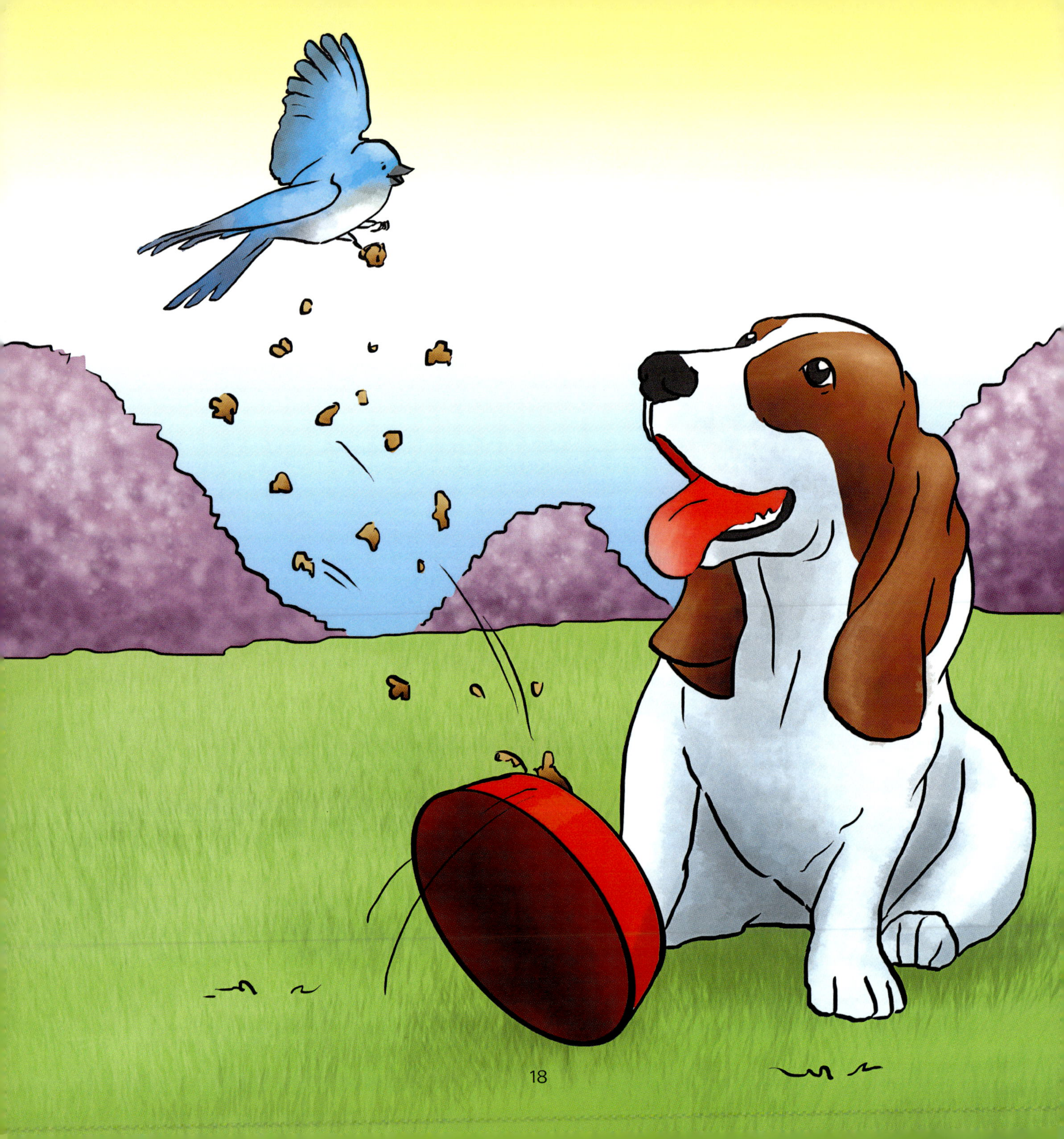

Max pulled the red wagon filled with food for the other dogs. Anna spared no expense when it came to animal food. She believed that every dog should have a well-balanced diet. Then all the animals, big and small, sat down to a wonderful breakfast of healthy grains, fruits, berries, and vegetables. Anna sat with the animals and drank some lavender-flavored lemonade that quenched her thirst. The first to be fed were the older dogs. The younger dogs had to sit until they were finished. It was important for the puppies to show respect to their elders.

When the older dogs had finished, Anna placed a food bowl in front of each puppy. No puppy was allowed to eat until everyone had a bowl. Then Anna would say, "You may eat."

Checkers, the Basset Hound, slapped his paw into the bowl. Food went flying everywhere. The birds flew in to snatch a piece of kibble, while all the other dogs laughed.

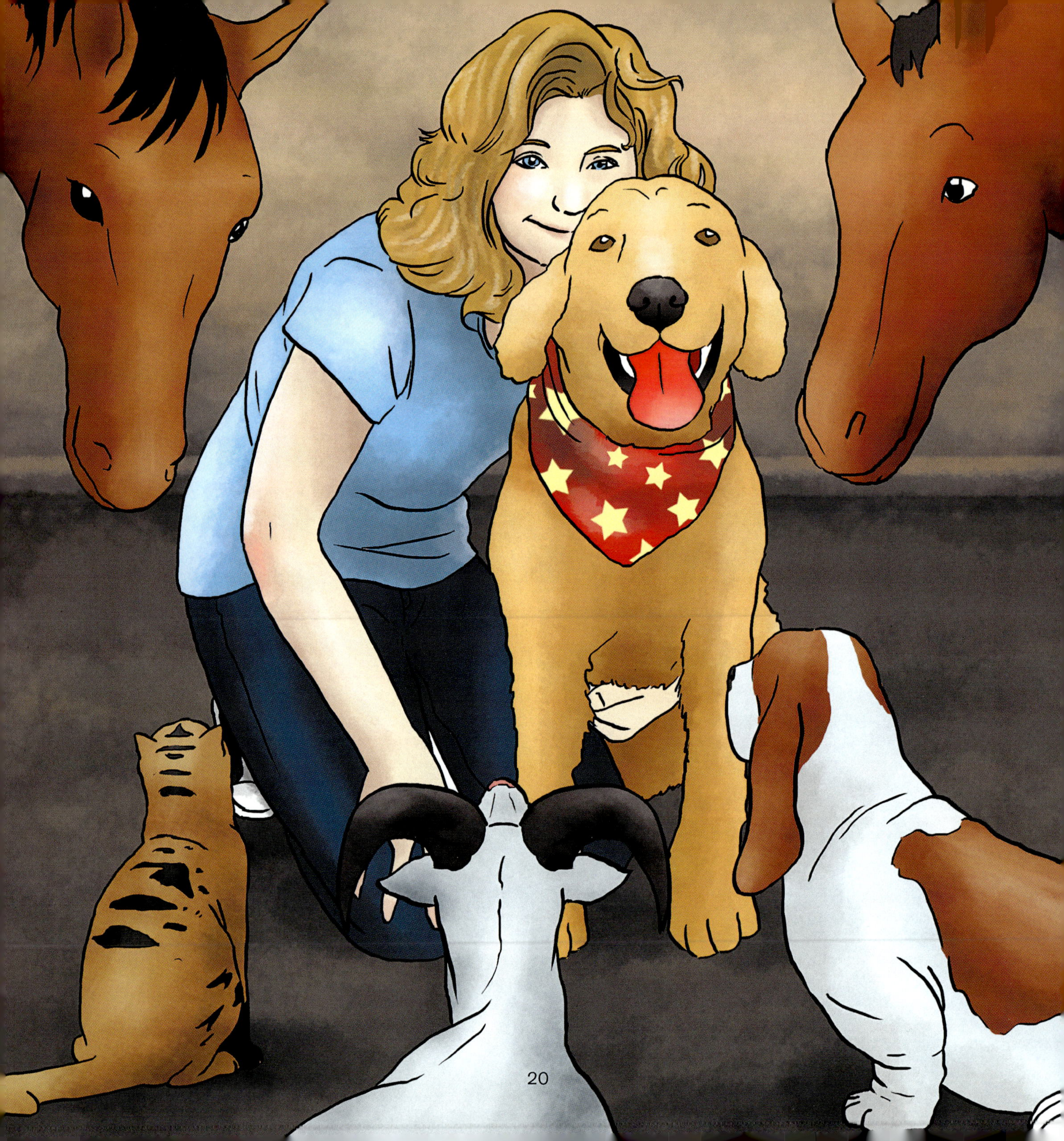

After breakfast, all the dogs gathered together. Anna believed every dog should feel like a member of the pack. Anna had all the dogs repeat in unison:

Just for today, I will be kind to every dog.
Just for today, I will go out of my way to help another dog.
Just for today, I will not worry.
Just for today, I will sing for the entire world to hear.
Just for today, I will be proud of who I am.
Just for today, I will respect and honor Mother Earth.

And finally,

No matter how busy I am, I will take the time to make the other dogs feel important.

Anna told each dog to be *grateful* while they lived on Lilac Doggie Rescue Ranch because in *Divine Time*, each dog would find a new forever home with a special family who loved them as much as she did. The dogs, cat, and birds loved Anna and the lessons they learned. Little did Anna know all the animals considered Anna's Lilac Doggie Rescue Ranch their home. It was a place of love, happiness, and peace. To show their appreciation, the dogs, cat, and birds would sing to Anna each day, *"I will love you until the end of time!"* Then all the dogs would listen to Anna as she assigned jobs to each dog.

As Anna was talking to the dogs, Dante slowly limped back to his soft bed and fell asleep. His hip was hurting, and his breathing was labored. Dante was very good at hiding his pain so that no one noticed, not even Anna.

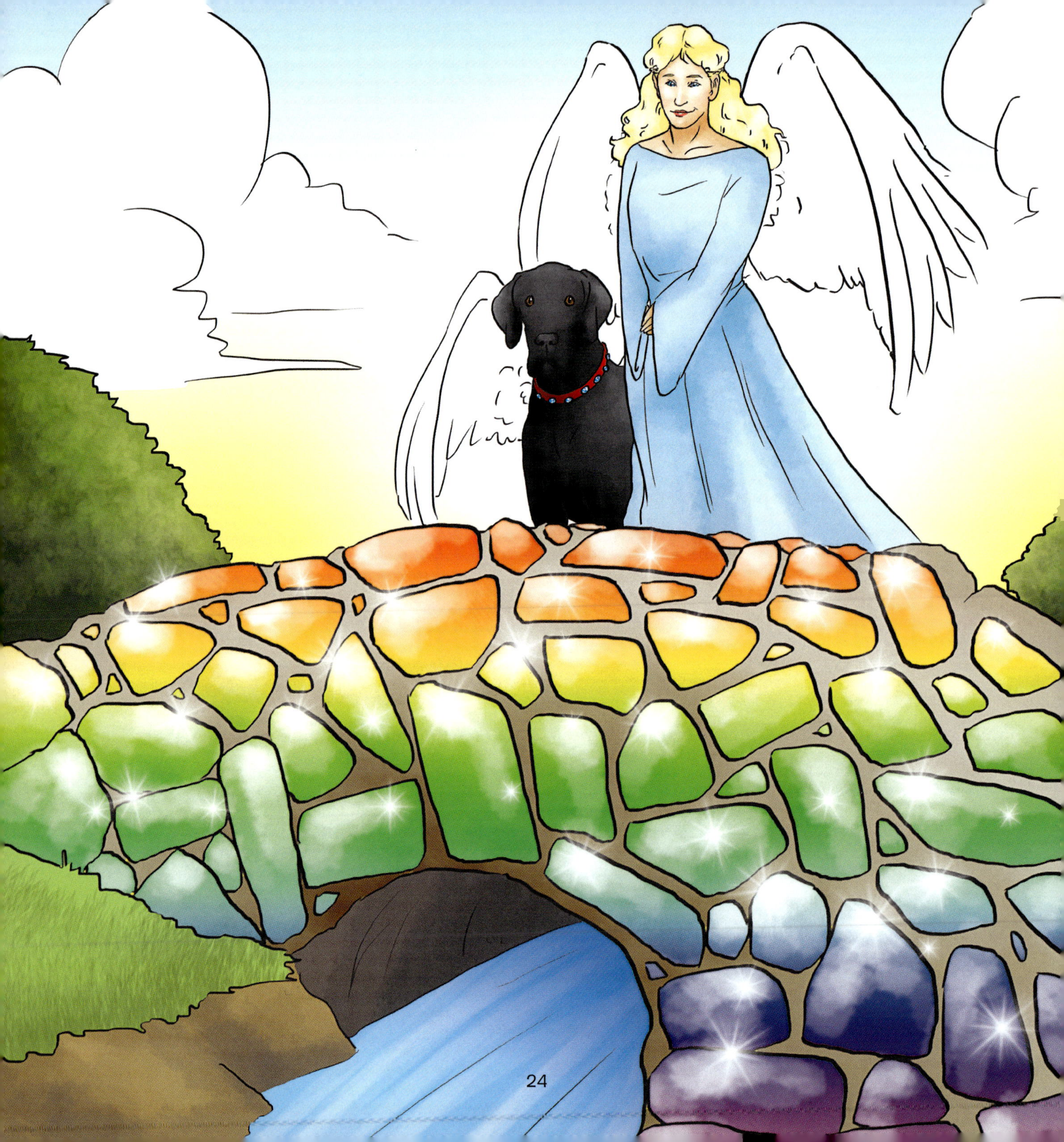

Two angels noticed Dante's journey on Mother Earth was coming to an end. His body was tired. Dante had loved and learned everything he needed to know while he lived with Anna and her family. The two angels watched Dante from Rainbow Bridge. The first angel whispered in the ear of the second, who just happened to be a Great Dane.

26

"My dear friend, Duke," said the first angel, "tomorrow you will visit Lilac Doggie Rescue Ranch and teach what *Divine Time* and being *grateful* mean to all the animals that live there."

"How will I do that?" asked Duke. "I am only a dog."

"You are a very special dog," replied the angel. "You were loved so much by all the animals that have crossed over Rainbow Bridge. They chose you to visit this special place of love. You will help Anna and the other dogs understand when Dante chooses to leave with us.

"But remember, when you visit Lilac Doggie Rescue Ranch, you must tuck your angel wings in your soft coat of fur so no one will know that you are a very special dog," the angel added.

"Wear this collar while you are here," said the angel. "It will keep you grounded."

The angel placed a beautiful collar with crystals that were black with white snowflakes on them around Duke's neck.

"What are these beautiful crystals called?" asked Duke.

"They are called snowflake obsidian," replied the angel.

"What a fitting name for such a pretty crystal," Duke said. "Thank you, angel."

The angel bent down and kissed Duke goodbye, and he crossed over Rainbow Bridge as the morning sun rose in the sky.

Welcome to
Lilac Doggie Rescue Ranch
ALL WHO ENTER THIS RANCH
MUST SHOW LOVE, RESPECT
AND KINDNESS TO THE
ANIMALS THAT LIVE HERE.

Duke stood by the gate of Lilac Doggie Rescue Ranch. He began to bark. "WOOF, WOOF, WOOF," bellowed Duke.

Anna was busy cleaning the dog beds at the ranch and picking up the all the doggie toys. Max ran up to her and barked. Anna knew someone must be at the gate because Max was always the greeter of a new guest.

Anna put on her helmet and rode her skateboard as Max ran down to the gate to see who was there.

Max looked up at Anna and barked, "What is that?"

"He must be lost," replied Anna and opened the gate to let the Great Dane in.

"He's no dog," said Max. "He must be a small horse."

"Silly, Max," replied Anna. "He is a Great Dane, and he told me his name is Duke. Come with us, Duke, and share some breakfast. All dogs are welcome here."

32

Duke followed behind Max and entered the ranch. Everywhere Duke looked there were different colors of lilacs. The fragrance of the lilacs surrounded Duke. It was so familiar to him. It was the smell of love.

Anna introduced Duke to all the animals as they sat in a circle. Duke asked Anna if it was all right to go around the circle and have every animal, big and small, say what they are *grateful* for before beginning their jobs.

"What a splendid idea," replied Anna. "Duke, you may go first."

"I am *grateful* for the green grass that feels good on my rough paws. I can run around back and forth and roll around on the soft grass," said Duke.

Next came the chickadee that flew down from the rafters. "I am dee . . . dee . . . delighted to give my thanks to the blue sky where I can fly around and land in dee . . . dee trees to eat the sweet berries that grow on them."

The old cat, Buzzy, spoke next. "I am *grateful* for the warm sun for shining your light against my silky fur."

"This is fun," said the dogs. "We want to go next. We are so *grateful* for Anna and her family. They took us in when no one else would. They tended to our wounds, fed us, and gave us a safe place to live. And Anna loved us unconditionally," said all the dogs, wagging their tails.

The horses galloped in the bunkhouse and surrounded Anna. They nuzzled and rubbed her with their large heads. "We are *grateful* for the beautiful violet lilacs that grow here for us to see every day and enjoy the fragrance they give off."

And the thanks continued around the circle until it came to Anna who had tears in her eyes.

"Why are you crying, Ms. Anna?" asked Duke.

"I am the one who is *grateful* to experience the unconditional love that you all have given me," said Anna. "My purpose in life is to help you heal so you may find a new home. I find joy seeing each of you every day."

Duke suggested the animals should find a place to write down what they were *grateful* for. All the animals agreed that each day they would write down what they were *grateful* for on the walls in the bunkhouse for all to see.

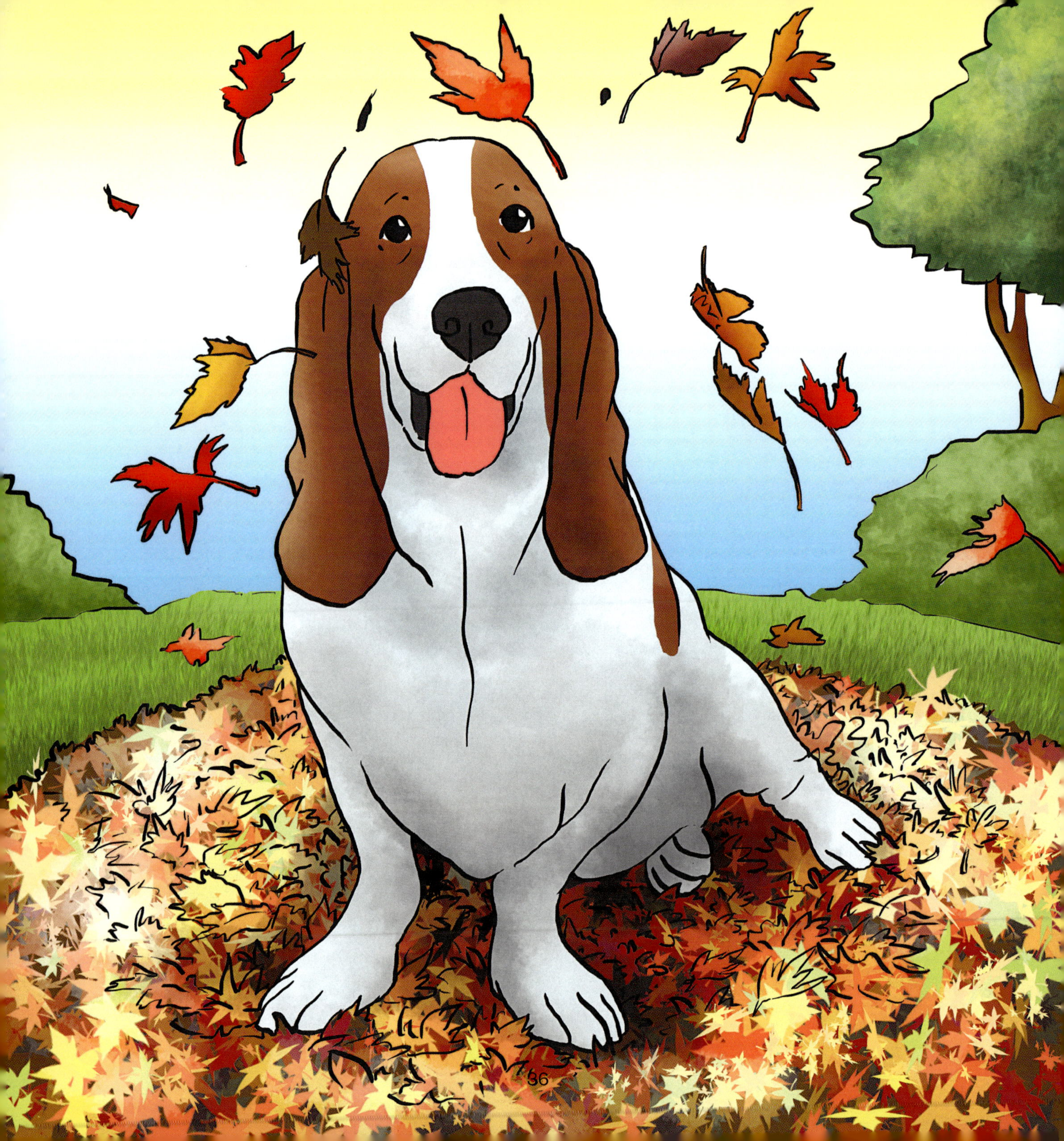

Throughout the day, each animal, big and small, did jobs around the ranch to keep it beautiful for any visitor. The dogs attempted to rake up the leaves into a large pile. Each time they completed their task, the dogs decided it was more fun to jump in the leaves and watch the leaves fall down upon their heads. Everyone, including Anna, laughed to see that doing a job could be fun.

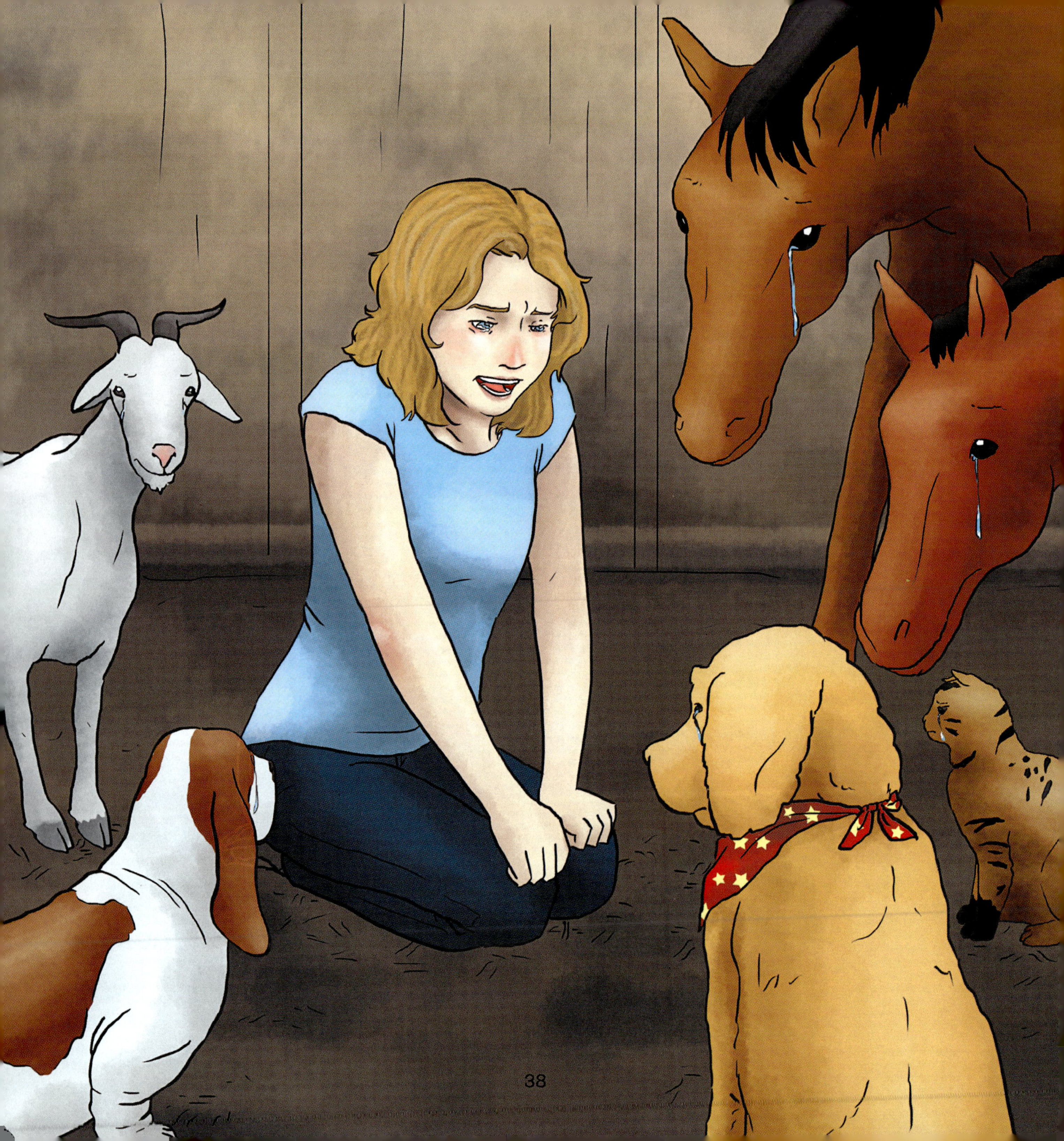

That evening, when all the jobs were done and dinner was finished, all the animals, big and small, sat down to listen to Anna's lesson. Duke sat at her side, showing respect to what she had to say.

"Tonight, my friends, I have some sad news to share with you," said Anna. "Today my mom and dad took Dante to the vet. He was not feeling well. The vet said Dante, our beautiful Golden Retriever, is very sick. He will soon cross over Rainbow Bridge. There is nothing we can do but keep him comfortable and show him unconditional love."

"When will he leave us?" asked the other dogs with tears in their eyes. "Dante is our friend."

"In *Divine Time*," replied Anna. "But until Dante chooses to leave Lilac Doggie Rescue Ranch, let us all show him the same unconditional love that he has shown us for the past fourteen years. Dante will know when it his time to cross Rainbow Bridge. A beautiful white dog will come to our ranch to guide him over the bridge. But before we go to bed, let us all repeat together what we are *grateful* for."

Just for today, I will be kind to every animal.
Just for today, I will go out of my way to help an animal.
Just for today, I will not worry.
Just for today, I will sing for the entire world to hear.
Just for today, I will be proud of whom I am.
Just for today, I will respect and honor Mother Earth.

42

Anna kissed each of the animals good night and carefully picked up Dante and carried him into her house to sleep on the warm soft couch.

All the animals were silent that evening, not knowing what to do or say. They had heard of Rainbow Bridge, but none had ever seen the bridge or the beautiful white dog.

Duke realized why the angel had sent him to Lilac Doggie Rescue Ranch. It was not to help Anna. It was his job to help all the animals, big and small, understand what *Divine Time* meant.

None of the animals could fall asleep that night. They tossed and turned their paws and claws, feather and hooves. Try as they might, the animals could not understand what *Divine Time* meant.

44

Duke gathered the animals around him to help them understand.

"I don't understand," chirped the chickadee. "Does dee . . . dee mean dee . . . vine on the tree over in the meadow past the lilacs? Can we visit Dante when it's dee time?"

"No, my sweet bird," replied Duke.

"Why can't we catch time in a bottle for Dante like when we catch fireflies?" said the horses. "Then Dante will have lots of extra time to be with us."

"We know," said the dogs. "We will assign Checkers to be a watchdog. She can wear a new high-tech watch around her paw so she will know when it is Divine Time."

"How about we stretch time like I stretch my body," purred Buzzy, the cat. "Will that help Dante? I could teach him yoga."

"Let me go out to the garden and pick some thyme, the herb," said the dyslexic goat who thought he was a dog. "I can chew off enough thyme so Dante can get stronger. I have a great recipe for 'Thyme Divine.'"

"Maybe we can slow down time so we can think up new ways to keep Dante with us," said the turtles, not wanting to be left out of the conversation.

48

Duke told every animal, big and small, each of their ideas was very good, but *Divine Time* means something different. "Let us walk together in the moonlight and ask the Wise Old Tree what *Divine Time* means," said Duke. All the animals, big and small, walked silently to the Wise Old Tree.

"Hoo, hoo is there?" said the owl sitting up in the branches of the Wise Old Tree.

"It is I, the Great Dane," said Duke. "We have come to ask the Wise Old Tree a very important question."

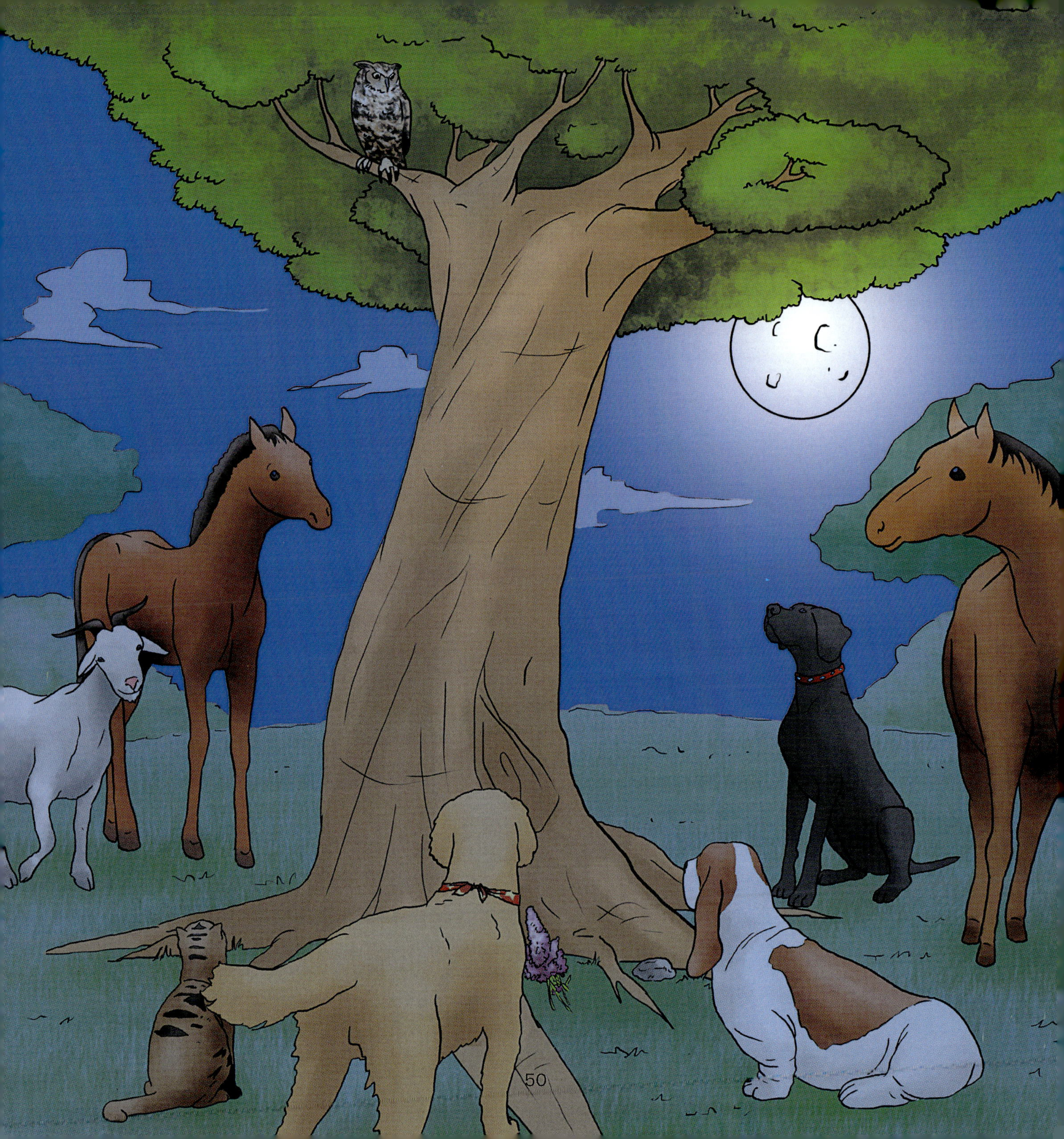

"I have been waiting for you," said the tree. "You have come to see me and ask what *Divine Time* means."

"How did you know?" asked all the animals, big and small.

"Because Anna came by earlier this evening and asked the same question so she could help you understand," said the Wise Old Tree. "This is what I told her: *Divine Time* means everything happens for a reason at the right time."

"I still don't understand," said one brave dog. "Dante is our friend. He makes us feel safe when there are storms. Who will do that if he leaves us?"

"Time marches on," said the Wise Old Tree. "Dante has learned all the lessons he needed to know during his life. Now it is his time to be with all the other dogs and cats that have crossed Rainbow Bridge."

"But what about us?" asked the animals, big and small. "Doesn't Dante love us?"

"More than you can ever imagine," replied the Wise Old Tree. "But another dog is coming to take his place so Dante can be with all the other animals that have crossed Rainbow Bridge. Then he will be free of pain." The Wise Old Tree closed his eyes and went back to sleep.

54

The animals, big and small, followed Duke back to the bunkhouse. They all slept together that night with Duke resting his big head on top of one of the horses that sneaked in.

The sun rose the next morning. All the animals, big and small, stretched their paws and claws, hooves and feathers, and sat in a circle waiting for Anna. Duke spoke before she came in with their breakfasts. He tried to explain to all the animals what the Wise Old Tree was telling them.

"*Divine Time* means everything happens for a reason at the right time," said Duke. "The lovely lilacs grow here so you can enjoy their color and fragrance. But as we all know, the lilacs are only here for a short period. You can't expect the lilacs to bloom all year. You have to be grateful for the time they are here."

Then Duke spoke about Dante. "Dante lives for the moment. He shows unconditional love for everyone at the ranch. He has lived a joyful life and has left a paw print on all your hearts.

"But you can't force Dante to stay when his body is ready to cross Rainbow Bridge," said Duke. "When he crosses Rainbow Bridge, his legs will no longer hurt. He will be able to bark as loud as he wants. Dante will have the energy to run with the pack again and to see old friends. And in *Divine Time,* a new friend will take Dante's place to love you unconditionally. You will always remember the wonderful times you had with Dante. No one can take away your memories."

"That is not so scary," said the dogs.

"Will we see the Sacred White Dog?" asked Buzzy.

"No, I'm afraid not," said Duke. "Only Dante will see him."

58

The chickadee flew down upon the head of one of the horses and chirped, "I know what we can do. Let's have a celebration for Dante."

It was agreed—the animals, big and small, would celebrate Dante in their own special ways. There was romping, stomping, hooting, howling, and laughing all night long with Dante. Everybody had a chance to live in the moment just like Dante.

Finally, the dogs asked, "Does anybody know what time it is?"

Duke replied, "Time for bed!"

Each animal, big and small, cleaned up their messes before going to bed. Then the animals said in unison with love in their hearts to Dante,

Just for today, I will be kind to everyone, especially Dante.
Just for today, I will go out of my way to help someone because of Dante.
Just for today, I will not worry because Dante will be OK.
Just for today, I will sing to Dante for the entire world to hear.
Just for today, I will be proud of Dante for living in the moment.
And, just for today, I will remember Dante for being our friend.

Then all the animals, big and small, gathered in the bunkhouse and said a prayer for Dante. They found their special place and fell asleep. After all the animals were sleeping soundly, a soft purple mist fell over Lilac Doggie Rescue Ranch.

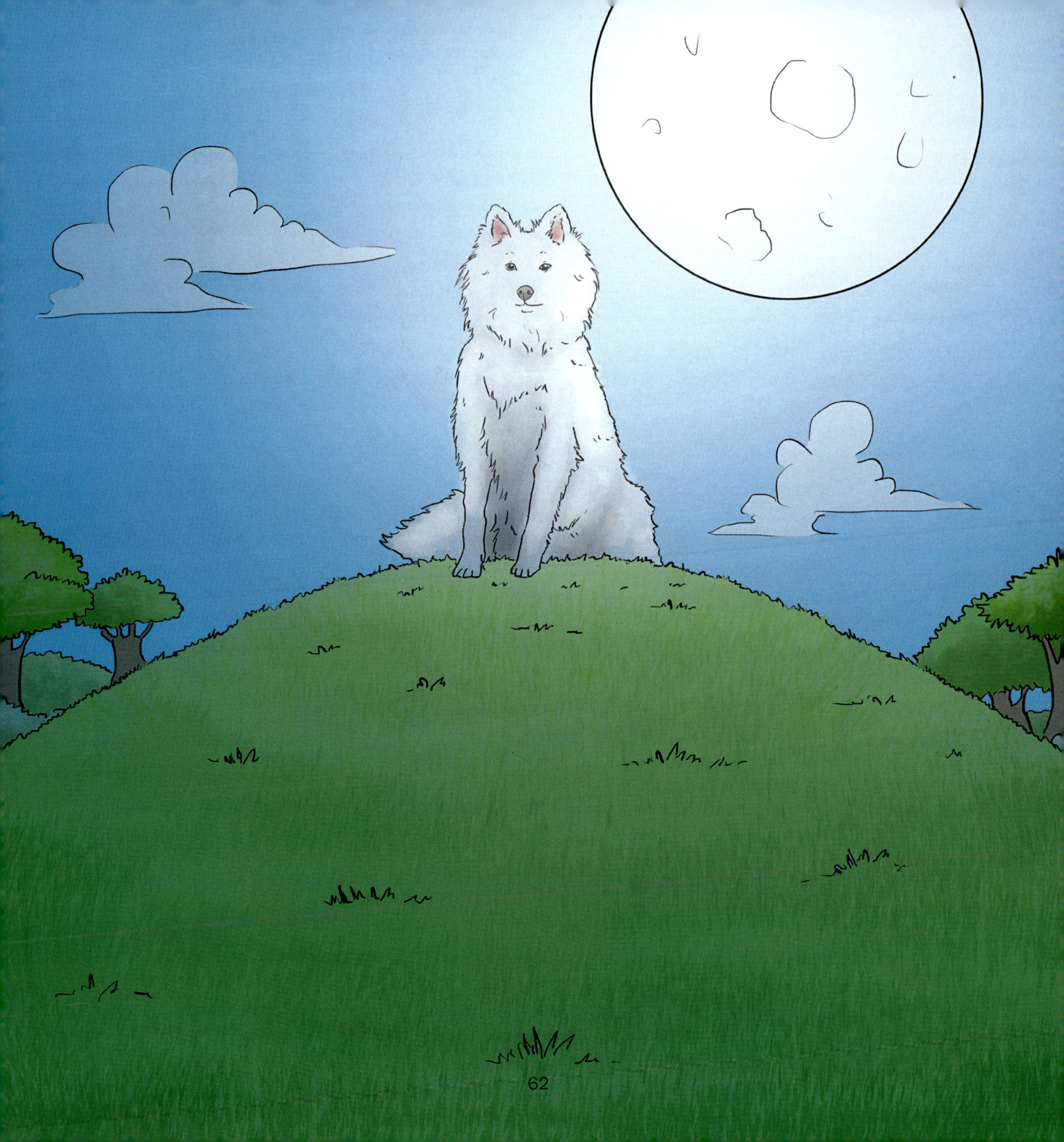

Duke walked up to Dante and said, "Are you ready?"

Dante knew what Duke was talking about. He limped quietly out of the bunkhouse and saw the Sacred White Dog sitting upon the hill.

"He is so beautiful," said Dante.

At that very moment, Duke's wings unfolded, and Dante knew he was really an angel.

"Dante, the Sacred White Dog and I are here to guide you to Rainbow Bridge," said Duke.

"Before I leave, may I write a letter to Anna and all the animals?" asked Dante.

"Take as much time as you need," replied Duke, now stretching his beautiful sparkling wings in the moonlight.

When Dante was finished, he taped his letter to the door of the bunkhouse for Anna and all the animals, big and small.

64

Duke and the Sacred White Dog walked with Dante to Rainbow Bridge. The angel was waiting for them. Dante could see hundreds of cats and dogs wagging their tails and waiting to greet him.

"You know, Duke, I did have the time of my life with Anna and all the animals that lived at Lilac Doggie Rescue Ranch, but I'm ready to go home now."

The Sacred White Dog helped Dante cross Rainbow Bridge where he was given his beautiful angel wings and was greeted with the unconditional love of all the animals waiting for him.

66

The angel looked down at the Great Dane and said, "I am very proud of you, Duke. Now I will give you a choice. You may stay here at Lilac Doggie Rescue Ranch and continue to teach, or you may cross back over the bridge. There is no wrong choice."

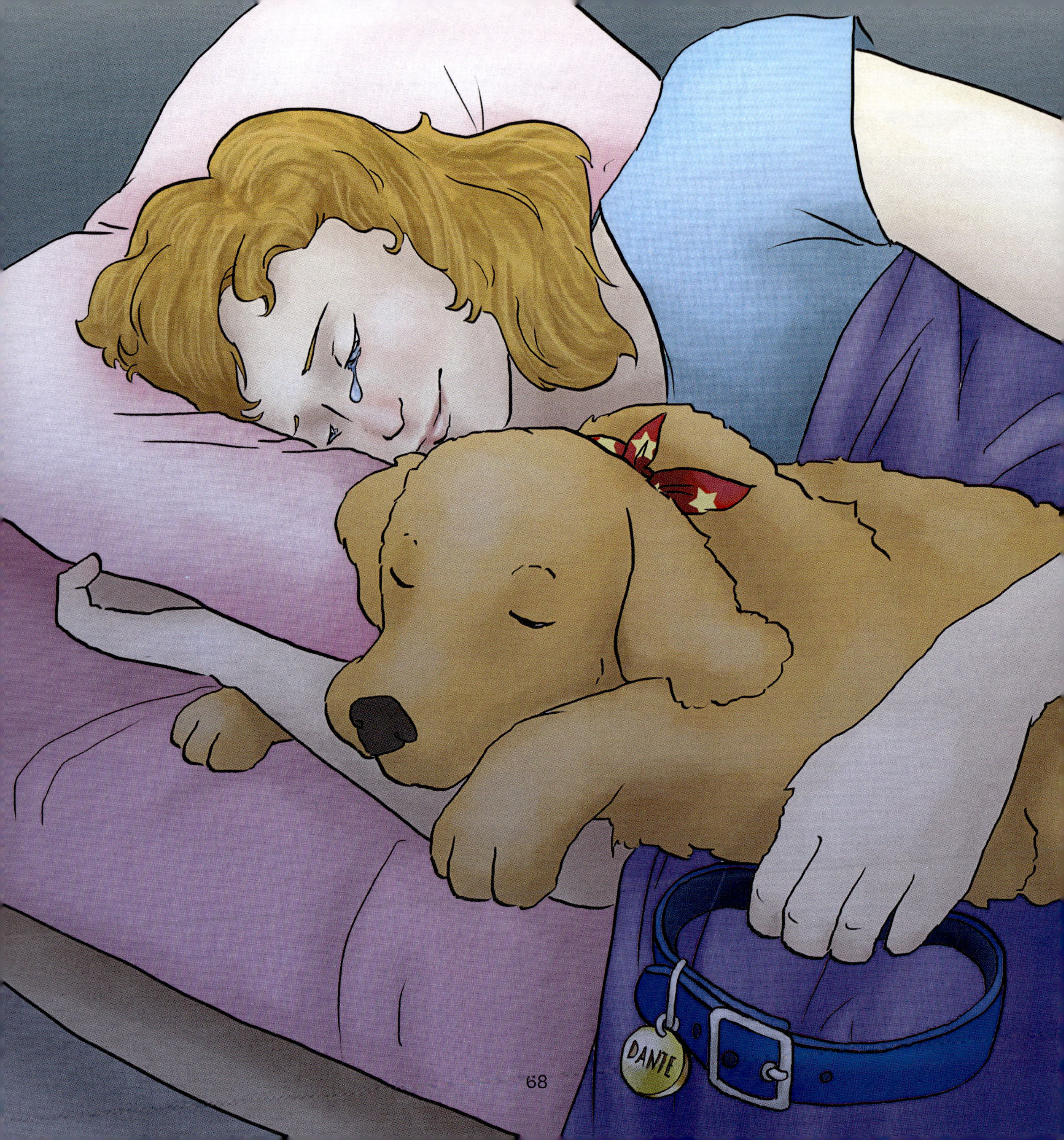
DANTE

Back at Lilac Doggie Rescue Ranch, Anna's mother came into her bedroom that night with Dante's collar. She held Anna as only a mother can. "Dante crossed peacefully, Anna. I thought you would like to keep his collar."

Max jumped up on Anna's bed. He pushed his head under Anna's hand, waiting for his ears to be rubbed. "What a good dog you are, Max," Anna said. "Now it's your turn to be the big dog. Dante would have wanted that."

Anna's mother kissed her good night and patted Max on the back.

The sweet scent of lilacs crept through Anna's window as she fell asleep. Max put his head down on the bed so he could be close to Anna as she slept. That night Anna had a beautiful dream as she held Dante's collar. She saw a land filled with love, light, and happiness. She could feel unconditional love flowing through her body. Dante was running with no pain across a beautiful meadow filled with multicolored flowers she had never seen.

When he stopped running, Dante looked at Anna and said, *"Thank you, Anna. I will love you to the end of time."*

Then Dante and all the animals, big and small, sang, *"I had the time of my life because of you, Anna."* And they did! A tear of happiness fell down Anna's cheek. She smiled, knowing Dante was OK.

So, readers, it's up to you to finish the story. Does Duke, the Great Dane, stay at the ranch to continue helping Anna, or does he cross back over Rainbow Bridge? There are no wrong choices. And you have all the time you need to finish this story, for as you know, now you may have *the time of your life* writing the ending or perhaps the beginning.

And what about the letter Dante wrote and left on the door. What did Dante write to Anna and all the animals before leaving? Once again, it's up to you because there are no wrong words.

But, readers, before I leave you, here are some important things to remember as you grow up:

- *Stand tall and be proud of who you are.*
- *Go out on a limb to help someone, be it an animal or a man.*
- *Remember your roots so that you may always be grounded, and respect what nature has given you.*
- *Drink plenty of water so that you will always be healthy.*
- *Be content with your natural beauty and that of others.*
- *Show kindness to all the animals, big and small, and in return, you will teach other people to do the same.*

And finally, *have the time of your life* in school learning. And remember:
- *Just for today, I will be kind to everyone in school and at home.*
- *Just for today, I will go out of my way to help someone in school or in my community.*
- *Just for today, I will not worry that I'm not smart enough. I am.*
- *Just for today, I will sing for the entire world to hear because I have a beautiful voice.*
- *Just for today, I will be proud of who I am and where I came from.*
- *Just for today, I will show respect to my parents, friends, teachers, and Mother Earth.*

Life is short. It is this very moment we should live and enjoy. Laughter makes the heart sing!

The Beginning

(Dante's Letter)
Dear Anna and all animals, big and small,

Love,

Dante

Edwards Brothers Malloy
Oxnard, CA USA
August 11, 2015